Beware, Take Care

Fun and Spooky Poems by
LILIAN MOORE

Illustrated by
HOWARD FINE

Henry Holt and Company ✦ New York

The following poems first appeared in *Spooky Rhymes and Riddles* by Lilian Moore
(New York: Scholastic, 1972): THERE WAS AN EGG; SOMETHING IS THERE;
THE GHOST IN OUR APARTMENT HOUSE; THE GHOST GOES TO THE SUPERMARKET;
THE MONSTER'S BIRTHDAY; POP GOES THE DRAGON (from "Spooky Limericks");
THE MONSTER'S PET; JOHNNY DREW A MONSTER; and TEENY TINY GHOST.
The following poems first appeared in *See My Lovely Poison Ivy* by Lilian Moore
(New York: Atheneum, 1975): LOST AND FOUND; SAID THE MONSTER;
WHOOO?; FOOTPRINTS; and WHY?

Henry Holt and Company, LLC
Publishers since 1866
175 Fifth Avenue
New York, New York 10010
www.henryholtchildrensbooks.com

Henry Holt® is a registered trademark of Henry Holt and Company, LLC.
Text copyright © 2006 by the Estate of Lilian Moore
Illustrations copyright © 2006 by Howard Fine
All rights reserved.
Distributed in Canada by H. B. Fenn and Company Ltd.

Library of Congress Cataloging-in-Publication Data
Moore, Lilian.
Beware, take care: fun and spooky poems / by Lilian Moore ; illustrated by Howard Fine.—1st ed.
p.   cm.
ISBN-13: 978-0-8050-6917-4 / ISBN-10: 0-8050-6917-8
1. Children's poetry, American. 2. Supernatural—Juvenile poetry. 3. Monsters—Juvenile poetry.
4. Horror—Juvenile poetry. 5. Fear—Juvenile poetry. I. Fine, Howard, ill. II. Title.
PS3563.O622B49 2006   811'.54—dc22   2005020257

First Edition—2006 / Designed by Patrick Collins   *9679*
The artist used charcoal and gouache on 140-lb. Fabriano
hot-pressed watercolor paper to create the illustrations for this book.
Printed in the United States of America on acid-free paper. ∞

10 9 8 7 6 5 4 3 2 1

To Marian Reiner
and to my young friend
Mira Kraft who helped
—L. M.

For Max
and his mommy, Tammy
—H. F.

There Was an Egg

There was an egg that grew and grew.
What was inside? No one knew.

It grew and grew, big as a hat,
Big as a house, and bigger than that.

Oh, what a CRACK was heard one day!
People screamed and ran away.

They tiptoed back and found the shell.
What hatched out? They couldn't tell!

And no one knows.
Do you suppose . . .

Something Is There

Something is there
   There on the stair,
      Coming down
         Coming down
            Stepping with care.
         Coming down
            Coming down
               Slinkety-sly.

Something is coming and wants to get by.

The Ghost in Our Apartment House

The ghost
In our apartment house
Makes EVERYBODY
Late.

He gets into the
Elevator,
Closes the
Gate,
Presses all the
Buttons
From one to
Eight,

Rides
Up
And
Down
And
Up
And
Down

While all the people
Wait.

Lost and Found

LOST:
A Wizard's loving pet.
Rather longish.
Somewhat scaly.
May be hungry or
Upset.
Please feed daily.

P.S. Reward.

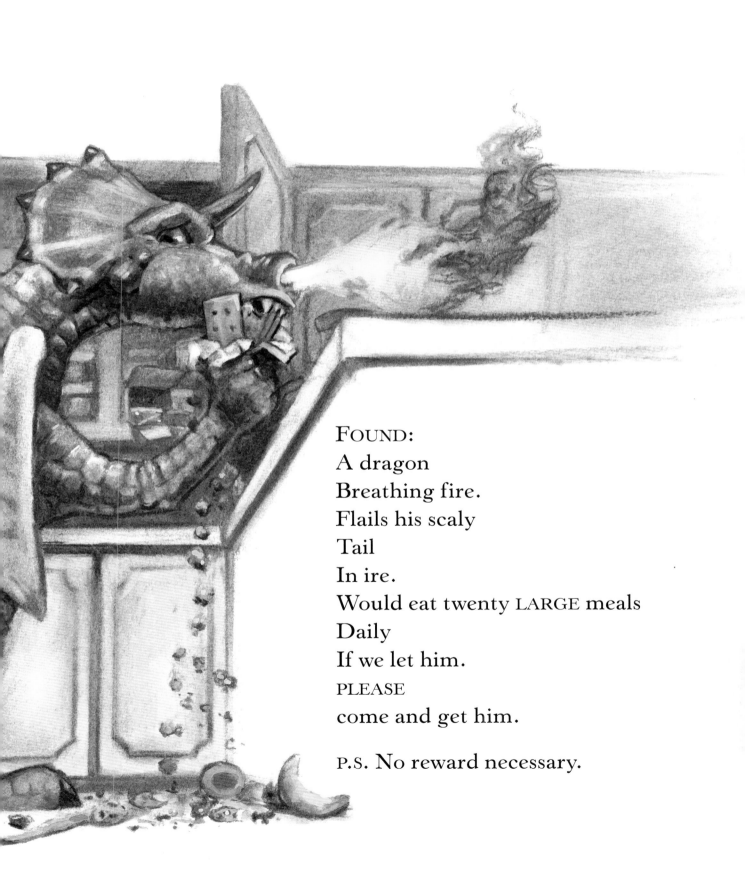

FOUND:
A dragon
Breathing fire.
Flails his scaly
Tail
In ire.
Would eat twenty LARGE meals
Daily
If we let him.
PLEASE
come and get him.

P.S. No reward necessary.

The Ghost Goes to the Supermarket

Whang! go the soup cans.
Thump! the potatoes.
Slurp! goes the syrup.
Squish! the tomatoes.

The soda pop slops.
The popcorn scrunches.
The jelly beans bounce.
The sugar crunches.

"I'm just looking for the toast,"
Says the ghost.

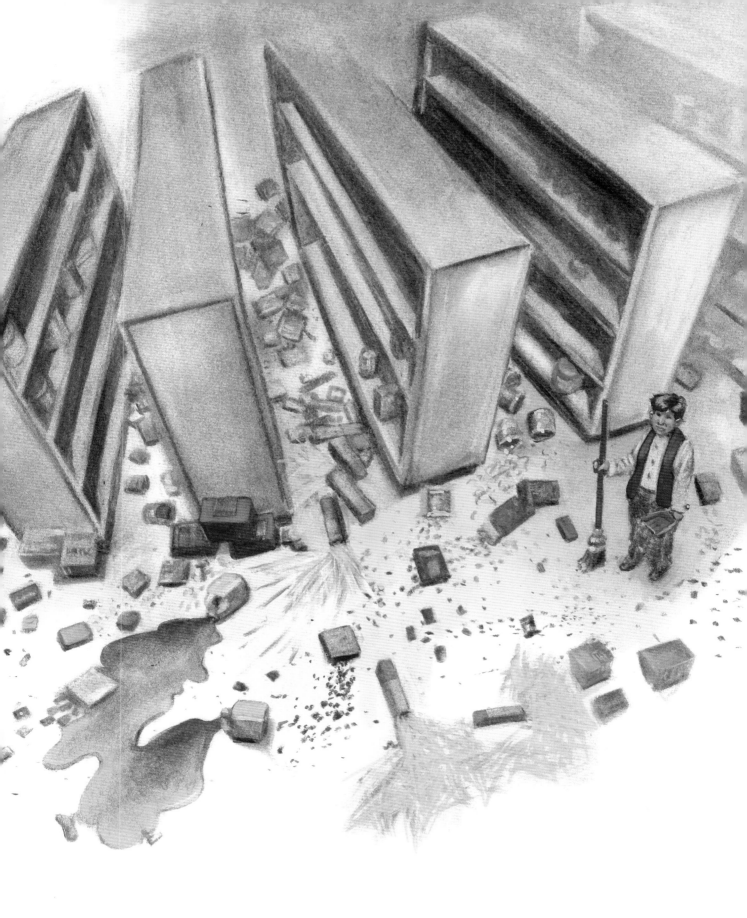

Said the Monster

Said the Monster, "You all think that I
Love to lunch on the folks who go by.
    If only you knew
    I'd much rather chew
On a peppery cheese pizza pie!"

The Monster's Birthday

Oh, what a party!
They all ate hearty
Of elegant bellyache stew.

Then came the cake
In the shape of a snake
And trimmed with octopus goo.

The balloons all went *bang!*
And everyone sang,
"Happy birthday, dear Monster, to you."

Pop Goes the Dragon

A Dragon whose size was quite whopping
Breathed fire all day without stopping.
   No child seemed to mind
   For he really was kind
And kept all the popcorn a-popping.

The Monster's Pet

What kind of pet
Would a monster get
If a monster set
His mind on a pet?

Would it snuffle and wuffle
Or snackle and snore?
Would it slither and dither
Or rattle and roar?

Would it dribble and bribble
In manner horr-ible
Or squibble and squirm
Like a worm?

And every day
In pleasant weather,
Would they go out
For a walk together?

Fog

Beware,
Take care!

Witch's weather
Today!

Misty
Twisty
Hide-the-way
Gray,

A poke-through
Wall
Of
Nothing at all.

Look ahead,
Look behind you.
Still no one will
Find you!

WHOOO?

Who . . . ooo?
Said the owl
In the dark old tree.

Wheeeeeeeeeeee!
Said the wind
With a howl.
Wheeeeeeeeeee!

Who . . . oooooo?
Wheeeee . . . eeee!

Whoooooo?
Wheeeeeee!

They didn't
Scare
Each other,
But they did
Scare
Whooo?
Me!

Footprints

It was snowing
Last night,
And today
I can see who came
This way.

A dog ran lightly here,
And a cat.
A rabbit hopped by and—
What was THAT?

A twelve-toed foot
Two yards wide?
Another step here
In just one stride?

It was snowing
Last night.
Who came past?
I'll never be knowing
For I am going
The OTHER way,
Fast.

Johnny Drew a Monster

Johnny drew a monster.
The monster chased him.
Just in time
Johnny erased him.

Teeny Tiny Ghost

A teeny tiny ghost
No bigger than a mouse,
At most,
Lived in a great big house.

It's hard to haunt
A great big house
When you're a teeny tiny ghost
No bigger than a mouse,
At most.

He did what he could do.

So every dark and stormy night—
The kind that shakes a house with fright—
If you stood still and listened right,
You'd hear a
Teeny
Tiny

BOO!

Why?

Why does the clock
Go ticking away
With the
Teeniest
Tickety-Tick
All day?
And then at night
When there ISN'T
A light,
Why does the clock
Go
Tock-Tock-Tock
Tockety-Tockety
Tock-Tock
TOCK?